# RED MOON

Jordan van Steenderen

Published by

VERSE CREATIVE

Published by Verse Creative
www.versecreative.co.za

PO Box 51233
Waterfront
Cape Town
South Africa
8002

First published April 2012

Edited by Stuart Rothgieser
www.stuartrothgieser.com

ISBN 978-0-9921992-0-3

# RED MOON

---

Jordan van Steenderen

Published by

VERSE CREATIVE

*Author's note:*

*I dedicate this book to my companions and my grandparents.*

*My thanks goes to Jemma , Cheyenne, Chiara, Lola, my father and my mother. My biggest thanks goes to Dani Clarke.*

*You all helped me to broaden my horizons and encouraged me to keep going.*

*Thank you,*

*Jordan*

# LUNAR DIARIES

# THE DREAM

Three hooded figures ran through a cobbled street. Just as they turned a corner, the smallest figure stumbled and fell.

"Get up, Miyandrea! You need to keep going!" one of the figures cried.

"I can't, mother. I'm too tired! I need to rest!" Miyandrea sobbed, tears streaming down her delicate face. The tallest, Miyandrea's father, grabbed her arms and pulled Miyandrea to her feet.

"It'll be all right if we keep going! I promise," he said softly to Miyandrea. She found strength in his promise and kept running. They ran and ran. Every time Miyandrea fell she got up and kept going.

They were just slowing down when a huge roar shook the buildings. The sound of breaking wood and claws on stone made them run even faster. Miyandrea's mother fell and there was a sickening CRACK, followed by a deafening scream. Her mother was lying on the ground, her leg pointing at a funny angle. Miyandrea and her father turned back and ran towards her. Too late. Two wolves, the size of stage coaches, came thundering down the road, straight towards her mother!

Her father grabbed Miyandrea around the waist and pulled her back. They watched as the wolves scooped her mother up and tossed her in the air. She landed in front of one of the wolves. The wolf hesitated before picking her up in its jaws and tossing her over a fence and out of sight. "MOTHER!" Miyandrea screamed, struggling to get out of her fathers grip. "Mother!" she screamed again, tears coming in waterfalls down her face. She struggled as her father pulled her away. She ran with her father, tears streaming down her cheeks. "Mother!" she sobbed. They ran into an alleyway into the country. The wolves soon followed them, their muzzles stained red. Miyandrea could feel their hot breath on her neck.

SNAP! A wolf had her father in its jaws. He let out a scream as he was tossed to the next wolf, who threw him over the side of a cliff. They turned their attention to

Miyandrea, who was standing in the road, frozen in shock. Her grief slowly turned to rage as she watched them run towards her.

She was furious. They had just killed her parents. She let out an inhuman shriek and ran towards a wooden shack with boarded up windows. She ripped a board off the window. Perfect, she thought. It had long rusty nails. Brilliant for beating their furry hindquarters. That's exactly what she did. She smiled as they ran away, tails between their legs.

# THE WOLVES

James Surely woke up drenched in sweat, his blanket tangled around his legs. He rolled over to check if Arian was awake. She was. He could smell breakfast cooking. He managed to untangle himself from the blanket and get dressed. This was the millionth time he had had this dream. He walked across the room to the full length mirror in the bathroom. As he combed his black, shoulder length, silky hair, flashes of his dream went through his head.

As he showered, flashes of Miyandrea raced through his head and as he dressed into his business suit, the image of Miyandrea smiling right at him etched in his mind. He walked into the kitchen. Arian turned around and smiled.

When she smiled, his troubles and worries lifted right off his shoulders.

"Morning James, sleep well?" she asked in a voice like silk.

"Other than having that dream again, pretty well." James said, shrugging. Arian smiled "I'm making your favorite breakfast, Choc-Chip pancakes!" she said.

"When was the last time I told you how beautiful you are?" he asked smiling and examining her long, honey blonde hair, her perfect tan, her smile and her emerald green eyes.

"Last night, twice before bed." Arian said grinning.

"Then you, missy, are way over due," he said. "You are the most beautiful woman I have ever set eyes on and I'm afraid you can't beat me at eating breakfast and being at work by seven o'clock!" He said grinning.

"Game on mister!" Arian said, already at the chocolate chip pancakes onto her plate.

After a huge breakfast and a lot of wrestling on the couch, Arian beat James to the door and grinned. "Once again I beat you!" she laughed. James smiled.

"I'll see you tonight and we'll see who can eat supper and shower first!" James challenged. Laughing, Arian pulled the door open and gently pushed James outside.

"You can challenge me all day, but I will always beat you. Love you, now go make some money!" Arian said,

5

kissing James on the cheek. Grinning, James got into his car and drove away.

As soon as he was out of sight, her smile became an expression of grief. She walked inside the house and into the study. She pulled open a drawer and pulled out a huge, yellow envelope.

Inside was a sheet of paper. "Dear Mrs Surely," she read aloud, "I have the misfortune of informing you that you are sterile. This is a result of an injury to your birth canal and a series of infections in your womb. I must also inform you that the infection went to a stage when it completely destroyed your womb.

"There is an operation we can perform to take the infection out, but you will remain sterile," she finished, not bothering to read the rest. She hugged herself and started to sob. Her sobs turned to tears and if you were to peer in the study at that moment you would have seen Arian Surely crying on the floor.

That night when James got home he found Arian in the kitchen. He noticed something was wrong the moment he walked in. There was no smell of food or a smiling Arian. Instead, she was sitting at the table, reading a letter. Her eyes were puffy and red, as if she had been crying.

"Arian, are you okay?" he asked, kneeling next to her and putting his hand on her shoulder. Her shoulders slumped and she gave the letter to him, before putting her head in her hands. He read the note. His expression turned from worry, to grief and back again.

"Oh Arian, I'm..." He couldn't describe how he felt.

"I'm shocked too," Arian said. James looked at her and saw that there were tears running down her cheeks. "Oh James! I desperately want a child!" she cried, the tears coming down her cheeks in waterfalls.

"Me too, Arian, me too." James said.

# THE SORCERER

As she stood in the street, Miyandrea's laughter turned to sobs and her sobs to tears. Her parents were dead and she was far away from everything she knew. She had lost everything. Miyandrea sank lower and lower until she was kneeling on the street, crying her heart out. Her grief blocked out the sound of the carriage that was making its way towards her. She didn't take any notice of it until the horses were trampling all over her and the wheels of the carriage were crushing her. She screamed loudly before everything went black.

As Miyandrea wandered through the darkness, a horizon of light started moving toward her getting brighter and bigger until she was blinded by it. Her eyes fluttered open. She was lying in a bed that was too soft to be her own. She was in a room with a huge window, an oak cupboard, a red carpet and a chest made of fir wood. Standing over her and dabbing her forehead with a cloth, was a tall woman with black hair tied in a tight bun on her head, brown intelligent eyes and wearing a long black dress with a white apron over it.

The woman stopped when Miyandrea opened her eyes.

"Master, she is awake," the woman said, turning around and addressing a tall, old man, with a long, grey beard plaited over his shoulder. He was wearing a long, navy blue robe.

"Where am I and who are you?" Miyandrea asked.

"I am the sorcerer, Janus, and this is the beautiful, devoted employee and nurse to the ill and wounded, Mary," the old man said in the voice of a much younger man. "You, my dear girl, are in a castle, in the highest cliffs, were the sun and the moon meet, in Ireland," he said, with a small smile.

"How did I come to be here?" Miyandrea asked.

"We found you on my Master's evening walk, lying on the street, covered in blood and barely breathing." Mary said, worry shining brightly in her eyes. "We rushed you home and cleaned your wounds. My Master said that destiny brought you here because of your gifts." Mary smiled

"What gifts?" Miyandrea asked.

"You, my dear, are one of the rare children who have been picked by the supernatural to carry a gift and keep that gift living. For instance, a vampire will bite to keep immortality alive. Werewolves will also bite or breed to keep their race alive, and so on and so forth."

Miyandrea stared at the ceiling and thought about her now dead parents, her now destroyed home and as she did so all her feelings and thoughts were swept off her shoulders.

"Welcome to Garasia, school of the chosen." Janus said.

# GARASIA

Arian decided to have the operation to remove the infection. James and Arian tried to carry on with life the way they used to but they just couldn't do it. After the operation, Arian didn't talk as much and had to be careful about what she ate.

On the 1st of April, James walked out the house and to his car. As he was walking he noticed something from the corner of his eye. He turned towards the rose bushes. A woman, about twenty years old, was standing in front of the rose bushes. She had long black hair, down to her hips. Her skin was olive and her eyes were startling green. She would have been beautiful if she didn't have thick scars running diagonally across her legs and arms. She looked strangely familiar. It hit him. She looked like an older version of Miyandrea and the scars would be from the carriage, but it couldn't be. That was just a dream.

He closed his eyes and counted to ten and then opened them again. She was gone. Maybe it was a trick of the light, he thought. As he drove to work, he argued with himself. He was so sure that he had seen her. "It's just a dream, it's not real," he said aloud.

Back at home Arian was standing out in the garden, pruning the rose bushes, when out of the corner of her eye she saw someone on the road. She looked up and saw two horrible looking men standing across the road on the pavement. One had black hair, startling electric blue eyes, a thick scar starting from the left side of his forehead and running across his right eye and ending on his chest. The other man was the same except he had no scars on his face, but all over his body. They were both extremely muscular and radiated power and authority. They both wore identically tattered jeans and no shirt, showing off their biceps and abs. Their olive skin shone in the sunlight.

Arian stared at them. They made her want to run and not look back, but she had always faced her fears without running, so she stayed put and carried on pruning her precious roses.

The next time Arian looked up they had crossed the road and were now right in front of her house. She ignored them until they walked straight into her garden. The power radiating from them was even stronger up close. "Good morning, may I help you?" Arian asked, walking towards them.

"Yes, can you tell us if you know Miyandrea Night Heart?" the man with the scar said, in a much kinder and warmer voice than Arian expected.

"I'm terribly sorry Mr..." Arian said.

"Night Heart, Mr Night Heart, but please call me William," the man said.

"Is she your wife?" Arian asked.

"No, no, no. She's our sister. She moved here from Brazil and didn't tell us her address, but we managed to find the area," William said.

"Sorry, William. You look tired. I've got some lemonade inside if you'd like," Arian offered out of politeness, hoping they would refuse.

"No thanks, we don't want to intrude," the other man said.

"You really wouldn't be," Arian said.

"We need to find our sister," William insisted.

"Okay, good luck," she said.

They left and Arian felt a sense of relief. She didn't like those men - however polite they were. She walked inside. Out of the corner her eye she saw someone but when she turned around, no one was there. Confused she went inside.

When Miyandrea woke the next morning she couldn't remember were she was. Then everything came back to her. Her parents were dead, her home destroyed and she had been found by a sorcerer dude after being run over by a carriage. She didn't want to get up. Mary came in.

"Good morning.  Janus would like you to report straight to the room of chosen gifts," she said. "I'll show you the way," she added more kindly.

Miyandrea dressed in the robes that Mary gave her. They were bright red and fell toward her ankles. Mary didn't give her any shoes. She then took her arm and marched her straight out the door, down a passage and up a flight of stairs. They stopped at a door with a dragon on it. Mary smiled and said, "Sleeping on the job?" The dragon opened an eye.

"I was having a good dream," it grumbled. It yawned and then " Password?" It muttered.

*"Phileas garactis,"* Mary said. It lifted it's tail from the door handle.

Mary opened the door to a huge hall.

Windows lined the walls and sunlight filtered through. Seven long tables covered in food were lined in rows. A stage was in the front of the hall. Watching the crowd on the stage and seated on strange looking chairs were fourteen of the strangest and most beautiful people she had ever seen. On the right was a women, whos skin was as pale as snow. She had honey blonde hair and a young and extremely beautiful face. Her eyes were like violet crystals. Next to her was a dark haired, extremely handsome young man with violet eyes and small, but still noticeable muscles. Next to him were two men who had identical ginger hair, huge biceps and chocolate brown eyes. Next to them were two women. One had black hair and blue eyes and the other had black hair with blue streaks and golden eyes. Next to them were two men. Both had pale and hard skin. One of them had a hole in his forehead from which a worm was poking out. Janus was sitting next to an empty chair. Next to him was a man and women. Both had blonde hair. The woman had green eyes and the man had blue. Sitting next to them were two men. They had whistles like dragons dangling around there necks. In between the tables was a line of

15

people. Everyone in the hall was wearing red robes and were dead silent and watching the stage.

Mary took her to the back of the line behind a very nervous looking boy. All the men and women on stage stood. Mary ran onto the stage and stood in front of the empty chair. All of a sudden every girl and boy at the tables stood and started chanting:

*Garasia, holia Garasia, Weya chasia,*
*Garasia, holie Garasia, tesa egabola,*
*Garasia, holie garasia, tesa carriya*
*Esh gisia, Carriya*
*Garasia, holie Garasia, desa esagah*
*Garasia, garasia, ouway hosem.*

They then sat down. Janus remained standing.

"Welcome!" He bellowed. "To the new comers, I am Janus." He walked to the man and woman with violet eyes. "This is Helen and John. They are in charge of the vampires - seeing as they are vampires!" He said, smiling.

Janus walked to the men with the ginger hair. "This is Peter," he said, indicating the one on the left. "And Bill," he said indicating the one on the right. "They are werewolves and therefore are in charge of the werewolf cubs."

The middle table started to howl. Miyandrea noticed that all of them looked completely human and they all had small biceps. Peter and Bill joined in. All the other "teachers" smiled. Janus waited patiently for them to finish. He introduced the woman next to them as Joleen and Sasha and they were Elementors. The table to the far left made fire and water displays. Janus had to duck as a dragon shaped flame shot over his head. The pale dudes with the worm holes were introduced as Philipe and William. They were zombies. They grinned and waved. The table next to the Elementors started shrieking.

Janus stood and said, "This is Mary. We are sorcerers. Next to me is Gareth and Jane. They are Shapheasmorphagus. Shape shifters. Last but certainly not least, Eryck and Erica, dragon summoners and riders."

These teachers and trainers will now match you with your gift. Mary will mark you. All of you will have your gift symbol applied to your forearm. This will be permanent. It is not a tattoo but a magic mark that will grow brighter as you grow. I will now call out your names."

"Ashley Orgaf." Janus bellowed.

Miyandrea watched as a timid looking girl crept forward. Janus led her onto the stage. Helen reached forward and placed her hand on Anna's forehead.

Helen shook her head. Anna went through every trainer. At last Eryck smiled at her and said, "Welcome Sister." Anna looked relieved. Erica put a gold whistle around her neck. Mary waved her hand over Anna's fore arm. She then walked to her table.

"Peter Allens" was put as a shape shifter.

"Gaud Peterson" was placed as a Zombie.

Finally Janus called, "Miyandrea NightHeart."

Her heart thumping in her chest Miyandrea walked on stage. Helen, no, Peter, no, Joleen, no, Philipe, yuck! No. Mary? She placed her hand on Miyandrea's fore head. Mary smiled.

"Welcome Miyandrea. You are a sorceress." She said. Miyandrea couldn't believe it.

"Thank you."

## THE MEETING OF MIYANDREA NIGHT HEART

DING DONG! Arian raced down the two flights of stairs, through the passage, past the kitchen, through lounge number one and past lounge number two. Panting, she opened the door. James walked in and hung up his coat. Arian then ran past lounge two, through lounge one and into the kitchen. It started to rain.

An hour later, James and Arian were so deep in a conversation about James' $100,000 raise that they never heard the frantic knocking on the front door.

Later as Arian slept she dreamt that she was sitting in a field of money, her belly swollen and a gravestone saying, James Surely. Her body shook with grief.

Her eyes flew open. James was sound asleep next to her. She lay down again and listened to the "BANG

BANG BANG!" of someone crashing into her china down stairs. Wait a minute!

"James!" she whispered urgently. James opened his eyes sleepily.

"What?" he muttered. All of a sudden he sprung up. "Arian, there is someone in the house!" he said. Arian rolled her eyes.

"No, hey James? It's not like I woke you up urgently because I heard someone downstairs."

James walked out the room, closely followed by Arian. They crept down two flights of stairs, through the passage and into the kitchen. A girl, about twenty, was lying on the ground, her long black hair was falling from its braid and her olive skin was flushed. When she saw Arian and James she whispered, "Don't move." She got up and charged into the lounge. James ran after her. There was a shout, a gasp and then a thud followed by the girl shouting, *"Egoraebaya!"* A flash of red light and an inhuman howl. Arian ran in and saw James lying in front of the couch. His forehead was cut and bleeding. She heard a bang and saw the girl fighting a ... giant wolf? No, two giant wolves. Arian grabbed the extremely heavy James and dragged him into the kitchen, but before she could go back into the lounge, the girl and the wolves charged into the kitchen and destroyed her spice rack. Arian began to see red.

"THAT SPICE RACK WAS GIVEN TO ME BY MY GREAT GRANDMOTHER!" she shrieked, grabbing her biggest kitchen knife off the wall. The girl and the wolves froze in mid battle and stared at her. Arian let out a battle shout and charged forward.

All those years of Yoga, Pilates and gymnastics kicked in. She sprang onto the nearest wolf and stabbed it in its butt. Blood splattered her clean floor and the wolf started howling. She then flipped into the air and stabbed the next wolf in the eye. The beast howled and when it slashed at her again she swung her trusty knife and cut off its toe. The wolf howled again and this time when it struck at her it didn't miss. Arian's breath was knocked out of her as she hit the floor. She rolled over and saw the wolf's paw raised over her chest, ready to finish her off. She closed her eyes and waited. Nothing happened. She opened her eyes and saw her kitchen knife sticking through its throat. Its eyes rolled back and it collapsed. The other wolf howled pitifully and then, still whining, it dragged its companion out the window. Arian stood up remembering that she had stabbed the wolf as she fell. She felt a hand on her shoulder. She grabbed her blood soaked knife off the floor and spun around kicking the girl in the chest and onto the floor, pointing her knife at her chest. James opened his eyes and sprung up. Arian dropped her knife and ran to embrace him.

After an hour of cleaning, Arian, James and the girl were seated in the lounge.

"Thank you for allowing me to stay tonight," the girl said.

"Don't mention it. Really." James said.

"Please, forgive me for barging in to your house and..."

"Trashing it while fighting a pair of giant mutts?" Arian interrupted, clearly still angry about her spice rack.

"Pretty much," she replied.

"I would like to introduce us. I am James and this is my wife, Arian. I think I know you. Is your name... Miyandrea, perhaps? I dream every night about you but I always thought it was just a dream." James said, clasping his hands around Arian's. The girl looked at her lap, her lips pressed tightly together and nodded.

"Indeed, my name is Miyandrea."

James leaned forward and said, "Is your surname... Nightheart and are you a sorceress?"

Once again she nodded.

James then leaned in even closer and said, "You went to Garasia, school of the chosen, you have a mark on your forearm to show it, you were trained along with many other sorcerers and your parents were killed by those wolves when you were still very young. Am I correct?"

Miyandrea looked up sharply and said,

"How in Horia the Great's socks do you know that?" She looked absolutely shocked.

"Yeah, James, how do you know all this?" Arian asked wrenching her hands away from him. James started feeling embarrassed.

"Dream about it every night," he mumbled. Miyandrea broke into wild laughter.

"No wonder! I've been sleeping next door to your house this whole time. Obviously you would have picked up some of my memories!" She gasped, in between peels of vicious laughter. "Your children would be amazing if you had any!" she laughed, but stopped when she saw the expressions on James and Arian's faces. "What's wrong?" Miyandrea asked. Arian stared at her feet, sadness and grief clouding her eyes.

"Arian and I deeply want children, but she is sterile." James said.

"An infection destroyed my womb. I had to have it removed." Arian choked out, putting her face in her hands. Miyandrea stared at them.

"I'm so sorry. I didn't..."

James looked at her and said, "It's okay, you never knew." He put his arm around Arian's shoulders.

"You can stay here as long as you need to." Arian said looking up.

Miyandrea stood up and as she stepped forward she collapsed, clutching her leg. Arian charged forward and caught her before she hit the ground. James knelt down and examined her leg. Claw marks began by her shin and ran to her ankle. She was bleeding badly.

"She must have got hurt when she was battling those mutts," he muttered.


A small girl with black hair and olive skin was running away from two boys. They also had black hair and olive skin. All of them were laughing. One of the boys caught the girl and started to tickle her.

"Take it back!" he said, smiling.

"Never!" the girl screamed to get away from him. She laughed and laughed. Eventually, the boy let her go and lay panting in the grass. The girl started picking daisies out of the ground. The other boy collapsed next to his brother. All three siblings started laughing.

"Okay, I take it back - you don't laugh like a duck, Robert. Not!" she shouted and ran away again.

"Why, you little witch!" he muttered, smiling and charged after her. The other boy shook his head and ran after them.

They ran into an alley. Miyandrea laughed as she came to a dead end. Robert caught her and started tickling her again.

"Help me, Phileas!" she laughed. Phileas smiled and started tickling as well. "Traitor!" she gasped.

"Having fun?" a voice behind them said. Phileas turned. A giant shadow charged toward him and bit him on the arm. He fell onto the ground, his body shaking and the blood draining from his face. Miyandrea started screaming. The shadow charged again. Robert grabbed her wrist and pulled her between its legs and they ran toward the alleyway entrance. Another shadow appeared at that end and charged for Miyandrea. Robert pushed her aside and it bit into his neck. He gasped and collapsed, shaking violently, the blood draining from his face and body.

"Robert!" she shrieked.

" Go," he gasped. Miyandrea turned around and ran out of the alley. As she looked back she saw the giant wolves howling at the moon.

# THE WISH

James woke to the sound of rain thundering on his bedroom window. He clambered out of bed and downstairs to the kitchen. Arian was sitting at the table, watching Miyandrea instruct the flour bag to pour two cups of flour into a big mixing bowl. She clicked her fingers and the fridge walked to her and opened its door. She waved her hand and two eggs flew out and cracked their yolk into the bowl. She flicked her hand toward the window and the shells flew into the compost bin.

Arian clapped and cheered. Miyandrea bowed and instructed a mixing spoon to mix it into a paste. James smiled and clapped as he sat down at the table.

"Good morning and welcome to 99.5 FM," the radio trundled. "Today we're going back in time to hear the hottest songs from one hundred and fifty years ago. Get ready ladies and gentlemen." An old waltz song came on. Miyandrea started waltzing around the room, humming exactly to the tune. She took Arian by her hand and started to waltz with her. Arian laughed. Miyandrea grabbed James and gave Arian to him. He used the moves from his wedding and started dancing. The song finished and an ad break came on.

James left for work an hour later. Miyandrea and Arian were talking about 'girl stuff' when the door bell rang. Arian ran to the door and as she opened it she thought she could hear something like a helicopter outside, except that it sounded like a flapping helicopter. She opened the door and nearly screamed. Peering into her house was a huge blue, reptilian eye.

"Back Tarius!" A woman shouted. The eye moved back. Wind buffeted Arian. She pushed toward her door, her hair stinging her face as it whipped in the wind.

A girl dropped from somewhere and stood smiling apologetically in the doorway.

"Hi, I'm Ashley Orgaf. Is Miyandrea home?" she asked.

Miyandrea came running to the door. "Ashie!" she shouted like any typical teenager.

"Miya!" Ashley squeaked.

They both charged forward and hugged each other. Miyandrea ran outside and shouted, "Tarius!" in reply

Tarius let out a roar that shook the house. Arian crept outside. Standing in the garden was a golden backed, red stomached…

"Dragon," Arian squeaked. Miyandrea was scratching it under the chin. If dragons can purr, Arian swore Tarius was. To explain what it looked like, it looked like a giant lizard, with small horns on its back and giant, thick spikes (like a triceratops) on its head.

It was golden everywhere except it had a red stomach. It was stretching its wings in pleasure. On the top of its wings was gold and underneath that was red. Arian laughed. The dragon then rolled onto its back, its tongue sticking out and panting like a dog running a marathon. Miyandrea climbed onto its stomach and started scratching its stomach. Its back leg kicked like a dog.

Ashley fell down laughing. Miyandrea slid off Tarius and onto the ground.

"What are you doing here? I thought you were in Egasi," she said, walking in front of Ashley. Ashley got up, wiping away tears of laughter.

"I was, until I heard that the wolves were after you again." Ashley said.

"Janus sent me to look for chosen when I bumped into Gareth." Miyandrea said.

"How is he?" Ashley asked, smiling.

"He is acting as Mr. Protective Dad around Jane. Her pregnancy is going perfectly, but she's getting sick of how Gareth is trying to baby proof the house." Miyandrea laughed. Arian stood quietly to the side.

"Oh, I nearly forgot, this is Arian. She's my host." Miyandrea smiled.

"Please come in," Arian said, leading them into the house.

Arian was busy explaining to Ashley how a car works when Miyandrea all of a sudden snapped up as if she had had an idea.

"Arian, did you know that a chosen, if given shelter and food, is in that person's debt? In my case, I have to grant you and James a wish each." Miyandrea looked excited. "And I know one thing that you want really badly that I can grant you and it would take a double wish, but you and James really want it so there is no problem really..." Miyandrea was clearly very excited.

"Slow down, what wish can you grant us?" Arian asked.

"A baby!" James cried. "You can grant us a baby!?" he looked as if he was going to explode with happiness. Arian nodded. The smile slid off his face. "How can we have a child when Arian has had her womb taken out?"

Miyandrea became deadly serious.

"It would be incredibly painful and it would take a really long time but using a simple spell I can make a new one grow. It will be in perfect condition but she still wouldn't be able to fall pregnant because it is a replacement and it will only allow magic to enter it."

She took a gulp of tea before saying, "The next step would be to use a spell to make your family and all your doctors forget that you are sterile," she took another gulp of tea and carried on. "Then I will use another, very painful and very risky spell to make you pregnant. I will have to take a copy of your genes so the baby will be yours," she said, looking at James.

Arian looked fit to burst with happiness. James was looking a bit worried.

"What is the worst that could go wrong?" James said smiling.

# THE PREGNANCY

Arian dreamt that she was walking along a dark, winding path. James was walking next to her. They walked through a door and into a glowing red room.

Actually, they were in her womb. A huge baby was floating in front of them. An umbilical cord was attached by it to the side of the womb. The baby opened one eye as they approached.

Arian woke up, confused. She rolled over to find James gone. She walked into the kitchen. "No one in here," she thought. She walked into lounge number two.

Ashley, Miyandrea and James were busy setting up a mattress, with lit candles around it in a circle. The curtains were drawn and the only light came from the candles. Floating above the bed were green, red and violet crystals. She gasped. James looked up and smiled.

"It's part of the procedure," he said.

Eventually, everything was ready. Arian got into a silk robe and lay down on the mattress. Under her robe, a belt with crystals was tied tightly around her stomach to keep her spirit in.

Miyandrea stood in a green robe outside the circle. Arian closed her eyes.

"I have to do the first part now. I can't guarantee that it won't hurt. The spells come in something called, Sagaro. I have to do five Sagaro before I'm done."

Arian nodded.

"Get ready," Miyandrea warned. Arian felt herself lifting off the mattress. She opened her eyes. She was floating in-between the crystals and the mattress.

She closed her eyes again.

*"Agaro Seyar Clusmos!"* Miyandrea chanted. A fiery hot pain crept into Arian's stomach. It grew stronger and soon She started to scream.

"Arian!" James shouted. The pain subsided.

"Are you alright?" Miyandrea asked. "If you want we can try some other time."

Arian shook her head.

"I'm fine."

"Okay, get ready." Miyandrea said. Arian tried to prepare herself for it.

*"Geyaro esayo calusario!"* Miyandrea chanted.

Arian felt as if someone had poured petrol into her bloodstream and had set it on fire. She shrieked in pain. Her head jerked back. She couldn't breathe. Somebody was crushing her lungs. She gasped. The feeling disappeared. She gulped down precious air.

"Ready?" Miyandrea asked, sounding worried.

"Ready!" Arian choked out.

*"Galactros evarious!"* Miyandrea chanted.

Wasps were stinging her. Her heart was on fire, her blood was being boiled, someone was stepping on her chest, pouring lava into her stomach, punching her. She screamed and shrieked. Her eyes rolled back in her head and she blacked out. When she came back into consciousness she was lying on the mattress. James was clutching her hand.

"Ready," she said, smiling. James was as pale as a ghost.

"Ready." James said, stepping back. She rose into the air again.

*"Sacaros Taractus."* Miyandrea chanted weakly.

Snakes were crawling in and out of her mouth, biting her heart and throat.

It went and came quickly.

Arian opened her eyes and said,

"That wasn't too bad."

James watched with a cold heart as Miyandrea raised her arms and chanted,

*"Orgasto Plotsue molorie!"*

A translucent, blue orb surrounded Arian. Her eyes flew open, her head jerked back. Her arms and legs splayed and her eyes once again rolled into her head. Her mouth opened in a silent scream. A gurgling sound came from deep inside her chest. She let out a sigh. Her eyes closed and opened. She smiled.

"That actually felt pretty good," she said. Miyandrea smiled. Ashley feinted. Everyone laughed.

"One more to go." Miyandrea said.

"Ready." Arian said.

*"Sacratio democratus!"* Miyandrea chanted, sounding and looking absolutely exhausted. Beams of light shot from Arian as if someone had poked a bunch of holes in her and then switched on a flash light in her body. She started twitching and jerking round. The light switched off and she became still.

Miyandrea lowered her hands and Arian gently floated onto the mattress and opened her eyes. She pushed herself onto her elbows and into a sitting position. She stood up, looking dizzy.

"Stop spinning around, James. I'm gonna be sick," she muttered. James laughed. Anna murmured something and rolled over. Miyandrea smiled weakly and flopped, fast asleep onto the couch. Arian lay down again and fell asleep.

After carrying Anna, Miyandrea and Arian into their beds, James flopped down next to Arian and fell fast asleep.

Arian woke up the next morning feeling ill. She charged into the bathroom and was sick all over the floor. She stumbled toward the basin and washed her mouth out. Her stomach started to throb. As she turned, she was sick on the toilet lid. She washed out her mouth again and stumbled into the kitchen. Her legs felt like Jello. Miyandrea was sitting at the kitchen table while the frying pan made scrambled eggs.

"Morning Arian. Are you okay?" Miyandrea asked, as Arian vomited all over the kitchen floor. Arian shook her head. It started to ache.

Miyandrea helped her to the table. "Your body is adjusting to the spell," Miyandrea said, handing Arian a plate of eggs. She gulped it down as if she had never eaten a day in her life.

For the next few days Arian experienced severe headaches, vomiting and cramping.

Finally it ended.

The next step was the hardest.

Miyandrea spent a week tracking down every family member and doctor with Arian and James, erasing memories. Eventually they got every one of them.

Now came the easiest step for Arian - but not James.

James stood dead still in the lounge Number One as Miyandrea instructed. Arian lay on a mattress on the floor in front of him. Miyandrea stood in front of them, her arms raised, eyes closed.

*"Fracturo Copius!"* Miyandrea chanted.

James felt a cold sensation creeping through his body. His vision blurred.

When it was over, he saw a translucent copy of him floating toward Arian. It got sucked into Arians abdomen like a vacuum cleaner. She jerked up and down for a moment and then charged out the room. The bathroom door slammed shut.

The next morning, James stood in the bathroom, holding Arians hair back as she vomited in the toilet bowl. They had a speedy breakfast, dressed and were on their way to the hospital in less than twenty minutes.

"Positive." Doctor George said smiling.

Arian and James hugged.

## SEVEN MONTHS LATER

The lounge was crowded with family members, celebrating Easter. Arian, James, Miyandrea and Anna were all sitting on the couch. Arian held her swollen belly. They had announced her pregnancy to the entire family.

Everyone had been very happy with the news. James and Arian had got the news of a girl. They had decided to call her Leah after James' mom who died during his birth. Miyandrea had practically cried when she heard that she was to be the Godmother.

## TWO MONTHS LATER

Arian was watching a movie on the couch with James when she felt something wet under her. She looked down. A wet mark appeared between her legs.

"James," she said. He looked down.

"Holy meatballs and spaghetti!" he shouted. "Miyandrea!" he shouted, panicking. Miyandrea came running down the stairs and into lounge number two.

"What is it?" she gasped.

"Arian's water broke!" he shouted. Miyandrea raised her hands and muttered something. Arian immediately rose into the air.

Four hours later Arian held her baby to her chest, sobbing.

## LEAH SURELY

I love the outdoors. My parents, Arian and James Surely, moved with me, Miyandrea and Annie to California when I was six. My dad, being a lawyer, has a lot of money, so he bought a big house, with two kitchens, five bedrooms, two stories, three lounges, four bathrooms and a garden with a white picket fence. Our backyard opens out to a forest and that's where I spent all my time before....

We'll get to that in a moment. I climbed out of my bed, quietly got dressed and put on my socks. I crept down the stairs, avoiding the ones that I knew would creak. I tiptoed into the kitchen. My mom was cooking breakfast. I crept toward the back door, takkies in hand.

I placed my hand on the door handle and...

"Where do you think you're going?" my mom said, without turning.

"Mom, morning, never saw you there! I was....." Mom turned around and raised an eyebrow at me.

"Coming to eat breakfast!" I said, grinning.

"Uh huh?" she said. "Nice try, Leah, but I have eyes in the back of my head. Breakfast before the forest," she said, placing a plate of flapjacks on the table. I hung my head and dragged my feet to the breakfast table. I ate my flapjacks quickly and before my mom could think of another excuse to keep me inside, dashed out the front door, hopping on one foot so I could put on my takkies.

I was running through the trees before you could say 'Leah'.

I found what I was looking for: a blue rope hanging from the branch of a tree.

I pulled it and waited. A wooden cubical fell from the tree. Shaking shards of bark from my hair, I climbed in. I then took hold of the rope and started pulling, hand over hand, so that the cubical started to go up. A few minutes later, it had stopped by a branch. Along the branch was a porch. I tied the rope to a tree branch, and clambered out. I walked along the tree branch and onto the porch. The porch had a door leading to a giant tree house. I pulled a ring of keys from my pocket and unlocked and opened the door. It led into a passage. I walked through it until I found a hole in the floor. A pile of cushions was next to the hole. I grabbed the top one and slid down the slide. I flew out of the slide and onto a pile of cushions in a round room. I was in the trunk of the tree. A long window, cut into the tree, stretched around the room, sunlight filtering through the glass.

A round desk was pushed up against the window, which looked out onto the top of every tree in the forest. A round bed was pushed against the left side of the room. I walked into the room and to a fridge on the opposite side of the bed. I pulled the door open and took a can of Coke from the fridge. I walked to a cupboard and pulled out a bag of Cheesos. I put the Cheesos and the Coke into my side bag. I walked to a set of drawers next to the desk. I opened the top drawer and took out a pencil bag, sketch pad and eraser.

On one side of the room was a door. I opened it. Inside were ropes. I tugged on the ropes until a wooden cubical came up. I climbed into the cubical and tugged at one of the ropes. The cubical began to descend. A moment later I was walking in the forest, bag over shoulder.

I walked to the river in the middle of the forest.

I sat down and reached inside for my pencil bag and sketch book, sat as still as a statue and waited, listening, watching for any signs of movement. A few moments later a doe and her fawn came nervously into the clearing. A moment's hesitation and the doe led her fawn to the edge of the water to drink. Quick as a flash, I whipped open my sketch pad and started sketching this beautiful scene, my hand flying across the page. In a moment I had the sketch. The doe and fawn hadn't even noticed this sudden flurry of movement because, unlike me, they had noticed a crunching of dead leaves and the swish of parting grass. All of a sudden a twig snapped and without a moments hesitation, they fled from the clearing. I sat there, my heart pounding.

A moment later, a teenage boy emerged from the tall trees and dense grass. Even though I was only seven, I could tell he was hot! He had gorgeous sandy blonde hair and evenly tanned skin. His body had well developed muscles, only slightly visible. I tried to crawl back unnoticed, but without success. A giant crunch told me I had stepped on the packet of Cheesos! He turned his head and smiled.

"I heard that. Come out. I don't bite… much," he said, a kind humor twinkled in his eyes. I shakily got to my feet and stepped out from behind a hazel bush where I had been hiding. He smiled.

"Why did you scare away the deer?" I asked, placing my hands on my hips.

"They weren't yours," he said, flopping down onto the grass, hands behind his head.

"No, but I was sketching them." I said. My stomach growled.

I walked to my bag and pulled out the packet of Cheesos. I ripped them open and pulled one out. I glanced at him. He was sitting bolt upright staring at my food like he hadn't eaten in days.

I laughed.

Getting up, I dropped the packet in front of him and told him that we would share. He smiled.

We sat there for about half an hour, chatting and complaining to each other about animal abuse. After a while, he told me his name was Michael.

We met each other every day at exactly seven o'clock.

I snuck out the house without being detected. When I got there he was sitting in the grass, his head in his hands. When I walked up to him, he lifted his head.

"What's wrong?" I whispered. The usual humor didn't shine in his beautiful eyes and he was looking deadly serious. "Who died?" I tried to joke, but he was still just staring at me.

"You have to go," he said through gritted teeth.

"Why?" I asked.

"You're in danger. You have to go!" He snarled. I gasped. His teeth were stained with blood. They grew into long fangs. He jumped up, and as he did his body rippled to that of a huge wolf.

I turned and ran. He roared and crashed after me. I ran, my lungs gasping for air, knowing I couldn't run forever, knowing I couldn't get away.

My eyes flew open. I was in bed, my blankets twisted tightly around my legs, sweat plastering my shirt to me.

"Just a dream," I muttered.

After desperately trying to go back to sleep I unraveled myself from my blankets and went to my parent's room. No one was there.

I went to Miyandrea's room. No one. I went downstairs.

I searched every inch of our annoyingly huge house and started getting desperate. I charged into the kitchen. Pinned to the fridge was a pizza menu, a shopping list and a few pictures of me (as a baby) and of my parent's wedding, but no note. I ran outside, desperate to find them. I charged into the forest and ran to the clearing where me Michael and I usually meet. He wasn't there. I charged to my tree house and still found no one there.

Then all of a sudden, "Surprise!"

45

Everyone I knew popped out from behind every visible place. "Happy birthday to you!" they started to sing.

I had completely forgotten that it was my birthday. I ran towards my dad and playfully started punching him.

"Help!" he shouted, pretending to be desperate.

"How is your dad supposed to give you your present if you're going to rip him into James Surely biltong?" my mom asked, pretending to be very stern.

My dad grabbed my waist and started tickling me breathless. Eventually my mom came and pulled us apart.

"What is a birthday without cake and presents?" she said, loudly enough for everyone to hear.

My aunt, Gazella, got me a huge set of tracing paper, sketch pads, canvas, oil paints, canvas paints, pencils, crayons, pens, chalk, spray paint and charcoal pieces. My uncle (my aunt and him are divorced) got me a stack of National Geographic Kids magazines (he works for the editor) and a camera. By the time I had unwrapped a present from everyone - except my parents - there was already a huge mound of wrapping paper lying on the floor. My dad then brought a picnic basket from behind the couch and placed it in front of me.

My mom put a purple wrapped parcel on my lap. I unwrapped it and found

A: A leash

B: A collar

C: A blue knobbly chew bone and

D: A dog bed

Confused, my mind buzzing with suspicion, I pried the lid of the basket open and peered inside. There was a blur of gold and soft fur and something leapt out of the basket, onto my chest (giving me the fright of my life), covering me with slobber.

"A puppy!" I giggled.

My dad pulled the wriggling rascal off me and said firmly, "Sit!"

Reluctantly, it sat down. I scratched its soft fluffy ears and giggled as it rolled onto its back kicking its hind legs. Examining it carefully, I noticed the characteristics of both a Labrador and Golden Retriever. Another very unusual characteristic was his black patches. Normally, Labradors and Retrievers are only one color, but he had black patches on his paws, ears and tail tip.

"We searched for a long time to find you a dog just like you. He's a mixed breed between a Labrador, a Retriever and an Alsatian," my mom said. "He is smart, obedient and full of energy. He also is a very strong swimmer." I smiled.

"What are you going to name him, dear?" my granny asked, hobbling over to scratch the puppy's tummy.

"Well, how about… Fluffy?" I asked the puppy. To my great surprise he sat up and shook his head as if to disagree.

"Albert?" I tried, grinning. Once again he refused.

"Odie?" Unsuccessful.

"Patch?" Nope.

I tried a number of different names and he refused them all. Eventually he got up and shot under the couch. A few minutes later he emerged carrying a model of a T-Rex. He started gnawing the head off. I had a lightbulb moment.

"Rex?" I asked. He lifted his head, gave a few excited yaps and then started chasing his tail.

That night I couldn't sleep. I had gone to find Michael after the party and he wasn't there. Hanging from a tree trunk was a long silver chain necklace with a small wolf dangling from it. Its eyes had been replaced with brilliant green diamonds and written underneath on its stomach was one single word, LIVE. It had disturbed me.

The next morning I woke up and, after a hurried breakfast, ran into the forest.

He wasn't there. Although I went to see him everyday, he never showed up.

# FATE

Being fifteen is cool but sometimes it gets annoying. For instance, whenever I get home from school and put on my stereo my dad always mutters "Teenagers" under his breath. Tonight I was out. My bag was packed with food and clothes. I tied a bunch of sheets together to make a rope. I then tied it to the bed post and dangled it out the window. I sneaked out my room and put a letter telling him not to worry and that I'd be back tomorrow. I did this almost every night.

Cool night air brushed my hair and arms as I jogged along Christians Avenue. Rex trotted at my side. I knew this was a bad neighborhood but I didn't care. I had become reckless after my mother's death. I could still remember her pale face, twisted in pain as she clung to life. Her voice choked with pain as she told me to take the small object in her hand. I held her hand all the way until her last breath. I had charged out of the house and into the forest, wiping hot tears from my face. That night I ripped the posters furiously from my walls, smashed the vase that stood on my dressing table and crouched on my bed, my head in between my legs. That entire night I was awake, crying into Rex's fur. Anyone who said that animals don't feel the same way as we do would have stopped dead in mid sentence when they saw the sorrow in Rex's eyes. While I cried he buried his nose in my hair and whined. Rex had grown super protective over me.

I gripped the locket that was banging gently against my chest. I turned into an alleyway and saw a group of guys leaning against the walls and bins. They got up and started walking toward me, wolf whistling and calling out comments to me. I stopped dead and gave them the helpless look. As they grew closer I smiled.

"Wouldn't hurt a pretty little girl?" I whispered, puckering my lip. They laughed. One of them lunged forward and made a grab for my arm. I grabbed his shirt collar and slammed him against the ground, then whipping up again I punched the second guy in the nose. Quick as a flash I unleashed Rex who had been bristling beside me just waiting to wrap his jaws around one of the guys who had threatened his girl. Not very long afterwards they were in a police car and on their way to jail. I described what happened to the police and they had taken in every detail.

I carried on with my jog as if nothing had happened. I got home at around about twelve o'clock and went straight to bed - or so my dad thought.

It was early morning as I snuck out the house. The trees seemed to whisper in the morning breeze. I charged into the shelter of the forest, my bag bumping on my back. I soon settled down between the towering roots of the water oak, as I used to call it.

While doing my maths homework I had the icy sensation of being watched. I soon finished the twelve pages of maths that Miss Lizardlover had given me.

I was just opening a packet of - you guessed it, Cheesos - when the birds that usually roost in the long grass by the river started flying off, crying calls of alarm. I watched closely. There was a crunching of dead leaves as something stalked towards me. There was a flash of black and gold and...

"Rex!" I shouted. The great oaf was slobbering me from hair to chin. He grabbed my packet of Cheesos and I had to chase him to get them back. Eventually he settled next to me.

I don't remember falling asleep but the next thing I knew I was woken up by loud barking. I sleepily opened my eyes. Rex was barking excitedly. I started packing up my stuff when I realized he was bristling and barking warningly.

I looked up and saw a tall, muscular guy leaning against a tree. He had brilliant green eyes and his hair was tied back in a short pony tail. He had olive skin and black hair. He looked strangely familiar. It hit me. He looked like Miyandrea. He smiled at me.

"Hello Leah. I have waited a long time to meet you." Before I could ask him how he knew my name he put a finger to his lips.

"Business is business," he said walking up to me and ran his finger gently along my jaw bone.

"Leah!" someone shouted. I gasped. I recognized that voice. Turning round I saw...

"Michael?" I whispered. He hadn't changed a bit. He still looked the same age and everything.

"You know him?" the guy behind me said. I nodded.

"Step away from him." Michael said.

"Why?" I asked.

"Just do it!" He started looking desperate.

"She's mine!" the guy behind me said.

"She is not yours, Orlando!" Michael said furiously.

Orlando smiled.

"I'll fight you for her," he said. Michael clenched his teeth.

"Leah, step aside," he said. I tried to protest but at that moment the roots of the water oak wrapped themselves around my arms and legs and pulled me down. I shouted in surprise.

"What are you?" I screamed.

"A werewolf, my dear. Isn't it obvious?" Orlando said, smiling kindly. "Don't worry, you'll be one soon." Michael stared at him.

"Over my dead body!" he growled through gritted teeth.

"Only too likely." Orlando said. I blinked and standing in the place of Orlando, was a muscular brown wolf. Standing in the place of Michael was a gray wolf. They lunged at each other, claws ripping through flesh, teeth clashing. The gray wolf was soon overtaken. The brown wolf limped over to me and was about to clamp its jaws around my arm when all of a sudden the gray wolf was on him, clawing pathetically at the bigger and obviously stronger brown wolf. Furiously he turned and bit down hard on the gray wolf's leg. Letting out a yelp of pain, he was flung against a tree. A ripple ran through him and Michael lay unconscious slumped against the tree.

I screamed and struggled furiously against the roots. The brown wolf let out a howl of victory and limped toward me. It pushed back my head and bit my shoulder, its huge teeth sinking deeply into my flesh. I screamed in pain. Fire was rippling in my blood, consuming me. It spread through my body and soon reached my heart. It started to pound, beating faster and faster. I thought the pain would never end. My vision soon started to blur until I was in darkness.

# FIRE

Fire coursed through me, closely followed by jolts of pain, ripping every cell of my body into shreds. I wanted to scream in pure agony, but I couldn't find my voice. I felt like I was being shredded by wild dogs.

My back arched, the fire stopped, but so did my heart. I choked and gasped, my lungs exploding and burning as I struggled to pull in air.

I felt a thud and my heart stuttered to life. I gulped down precious lung-fuls of sweet, clean air, blood flowing through my body again.

With the blood came something worse than fire. Dry ice hurtled through my veins, scorching me from the inside.

It traveled through my body like venom, ripping away my muscle mercilessly.

I found my voice at last and let out an inhuman scream of agony.

My vision came back, but the ice didn't leave me.

A figure was kneeling over me.

"Michael, please! It hurts, make it stop!" I whimpered, my lips cracking, voice choked in pain.

"I will Lee. I will," he whispered.

"Please..." was all I managed before unconsciousness swept me under darkness again.

It seemed like years before it slowed down. Very slowly, the fiery ice shrank back and disappeared.

My whole body sighed with relief - way too soon.

A spasm of pain gripped my body and made me choke.

This repeated itself for so long I actually started begging every God in the universe to just take me away, let me die. It didn't work.

Slowly, I got used to the heat and the spasms stopped abruptly.

Thoughts were brought to a halt.

There was a whispering noise all around. I froze and listened. Definitely in my head.

"Leah, Leah, open your eyes." A strong, male voice commanded.

"You don't think I tried that?" I snapped back.

"Fight it,'" the voice said, getting clearer, louder.

I threw an image of me rolling my eyes at it.

It sighed in exasperation.

"Curl your fingers," another, kinder voice ordered.

I felt around, trying to find my hands.

I felt a twitch.

Grasping onto it, metaphorically speaking, I worked to curl my fingers.

"Good. Good," the voices crooned.

I managed to find my eyes and a rushing popping noise rang in my ears as I surfaced consciousness.

My eyes fluttered open.

I was lying next to a stream, rippling smoothly between the long grass, over the smooth pebbles, pooling in gaps between the mud.

My eyes slid over the ground and I suddenly realized something:

I couldn't remember anything.

There was nothing there. Well, except the minor things like Maths, Algebra, Social Science, Natural Science and History.

I had no memories and I didn't know who the hell I was.

Sitting up slowly, I searched my memory, but I couldn't find anything.

All there was, was a name. Leah.

Suddenly a memory popped out of nowhere.

A giant grey wolf locked in combat with a brown wolf. I frowned. Why would that memory remain?

It was not of any importance, so it was pushed away. Taking in a deep breath I stood up.

It was a cold night, the moon hidden behind a blanket of thick, dark clouds.

The breeze ruffled the leaves of the fir and oak trees, making a soft whispering noise.

The crackle of dry debris alerted me to someone standing in the trees.

"Not someone - food!" the male voice corrected me. I whipped around to identify the speakers, but no-one was with me in that small, deserted clearing.

Another crackle sounded from a few miles away.

I shouldn't have been able to hear that but I didn't question it. It was completely natural to me, for some strange reason. A blanket of heat wrapped around me and a strange stretching sensation pushed against my skin. Leaving human form, I morphed into a huge white wolf.

I was surprised, but I obeyed the instinct to slide to the ground, a smooth, quiet movement.

I glided through the grass. A forest antelope came into view and I stopped, waiting.

My heart began to pound so fast all I could hear was a hum.

"Now!" all the voices were practically screaming at me.

I ignored them.

"Now! Now! Now!"

"Shut up! Shut up! Shut up!" I snapped back.   The antelope had almost disappeared.

Moron! Idiot! Fool!" the voices screamed and shouted at me. Once again I ignored them.

Using my long, silvery claws I began to steadily ascend the nearest tree.

All the voices gasped in surprise. I knew wolves weren't supposed to be able to climb a tree like this or have seven inch claws like sharpened daggers.

One paw over the other, claws sliding in and out of the soft bark.

In and out.

My balance was beautiful as I prowled the branches, barely making a sound.

My heart kept up the steady hum and I could hear the blood rush through my veins like a scarlet river.

Peeking through the branches of the trees I saw the antelope joining its herd.

Jackpot!

I waited for them to settle down.

Pounce!

Two antelopes spines snapped under my weight.

The other antelopes took off and I felt the thrill of the chase. I charged after them, yapping and growling. Claws extended, I wounded one. Its knees buckled.

I couldn't help feeling smugly proud as I hauled my catch back to the other two dying animals and came face to face with a bigger, older black wolf.

# SARCASM

It had its muzzle deep in the side of *my* antelope.

The growl that escaped my throat rippled and sent a silent threat towards the mutt across the clearing from me.

He (his scent screamed male) looked up, but when he saw me, went back to eating.

"Males are superior to females, so you are of little threat and importance. Anyway you didn't mark out a territory," an obviously male voice said smugly.

I let out another growl, my lips drawing back to reveal long, sharp teeth.

I was ignored.

Letting out a howl, I launched onto the male and began clawing at his spine.

He let out a yelp of surprise and pain.

Growling and snarling, claws raking the midnight fur, blood oozing from wounds, I fought him over my food.

Sliding under, I nipped at his soft and vulnerable underbelly, but before there was the time to slip back out from underneath him, he crashed down, trapping me under his bulk.

Squirming and growling, I managed to get out from under him, but he grabbed my scruff and threw me against a tree.

Small lights exploded in my eyes and my head was spinning. The male leapt at me and began raking my side with his claws, over and over.

I finally managed to skip out of range, blood oozing down my side, staining my pelt scarlet and stinging like crazy.

He lunged at me, intent on the final blow. Then he froze. I didn't see why at first and then noticed that there just so happened to be three arrows sticking out of his throat - nothing much! He slumped to the ground, morphing back to human. Shock finally took over and I morphed into human, skipping into the trees to put on some clothes, which surprisingly were tied to my left arm with green rope.

"Alright, who shot him?!" I yelled, coming out of the trees with my hands on my hips. At least 27 wolves emerged from the trees. Leading them forward was a girl, taller than me and obviously older. Her golden hair was plaited over her shoulder and a bow and arrows were strapped to her back.

Just behind her was another girl, her chocolate brown hair done in the same way. She was adorable. Her eyes were big and blue, her elegant little arms swishing back and forth gracefully. She was tiny, only up to my shoulder.

"Why, I do believe it was little Miss Sarcasm who did it," the little girl said, her voice sharp but warm.

"Oh, I wouldn't be talking, Queen of Midgets." Goldie said, smiling.

"Shut up," Midget grumbled.

"Any way, allow me to introduce myself. I am Fire that Dances through Forests, or Charlotte, and this is Lilly that Floats over Raging Ocean, or Lilly." Charlotte gestured to Midget as she introduced her.

"Come, we will introduce you to the pack." Charlotte said.

"What? No, definitely not!" Lilly protested.

"Yeah, I agree with Midget." I said, jerking my thumb at Lilly.

She scowled at me.

"On the contrary, you have proved yourself worthy and it is my unfortunate duty to make sure you get there," Charlotte said in a bored voice.

She had obviously had to say this over and over and over again.

Charlotte then turned around and walked away to end the conversation.

## DEW

The streets were slick with rain and a cold breeze whipped through the town.

Miyandrea, then only eighteen, staggered to the end of town and charged into the forest beyond. She soon heard a grunting and heavy paws hitting earth as something joined her. Diving sideways through the trees, Miyandrea wrapped her arms around the werewolf's neck, pressing her face into the soft, black fur.

He slowed to a halt as she started muttering in a strange language. She began to glow and change until she had turned into a magnificent, golden furred wolf. They ran together tackling each other and barking in pleasure.

Finally, they stopped in a clearing and changed to human.

Miyandrea stood in front of him, a tall man, his tanned skin and dark brown hair wet and glistening.

"Miyandrea, what is wrong?" he asked, placing his hands on her shoulders.

Tears welled in her eyes, pouring quietly and slowly down her soft cheeks.

"Please don't go! Don't leave me, Peter!" she choked in between sobs.

"Miyandrea, what is wrong?" he repeated, holding her face firmly between his hands so that she was looking into his eyes.

She took his hand and put it on her navel.

"I'm expecting a little girl to come and visit us in eight months," she whispered.

At first he looked shocked, and then joyful.

"I love you, Miya!" he said, wrapping his hands around her waist and kissing her full on the lips.

Miyandrea's hands reached up and entwined in his hair.

When they finally pulled away, Miyandrea smiled and gasped, "Her name will be Angelica, Dew that Glistens in Morning Sun."

"No." I said.

"What?" Charlotte asked, whipping around.

"You heard me! No!" I replied, placing my hands back on my hips and glaring at her.

"It's a miracle! Thank youuu, Lord!" Lilly shouted, raising her head to the sky and gazing at the stars.

"I refuse to come!" My voice was icy.

"I insist." Charlotte said, her voice equally icy.

"Why, are you scared?" Lilly sneered.

"Let me think: No and oh, I wonder, why won't I come? Oh, yes, I don't take orders from a sarcastic mutt."

I watched with a sense of very deep satisfaction as the sneer slipped off Lilly's face and Charlotte scowled at me, shooting ice at me through her eyes.

"Jeez, does nobody ever stand up to you bitches?" I asked, rolling my eyes.

A cold breeze blew up and the wolves shuffled uneasily. It wasn't the breeze itself that made them do this, but the scent on the breeze. It was like, how do I explain? It smelled like blood that had been concentrated with bleach and cinnamon.

"This is your last chance, pup. I'm giving you ten seconds to decide." Charlotte growled, unease clear in her voice.

I hesitated. A pack meant protection.

I slid into wolf, as did Charlotte and Lilly. Both of their wolf forms were a golden color.

A hissing, rasping noise filled the air and something huge and dark began to weave through the trees, just out of sight.

Our pelts bristled and fear was so thick in the air that I could feel it going thickly down my throat as I breathed in and out.

The hissing noise got so loud that my ears began to ring and I had to flatten them against my head to block it out.

All of a sudden, there was a flash of red and a black wolf disappeared into the trees.

His howls were abruptly cut short.

A few minutes passed and soon the fear scent was unbearably thick. I thought I would choke.

At that moment the biggest "snake" I had ever seen glided from between two fir trees. It had long, curving fangs and horns coming out of its head and neck.

"Basak!" A voice screamed in terror.

I dared not take my eyes off the snake to see the speaker.

The Basak's gleaming eyes picked out an almost luminous bronze furred wolf and hissed. The wolf flinched and the Basak struck.

# FIGHT

Charlotte let out a howl and immediately a message came to my head: "Attack!"

I had no connection to this pack, but I hated this snake and I told myself I was doing it for me.

Crouching down, muscles bunched I released them and wind and bark hit my face as I launched myself into a tree.

Looking down I saw the clearing in chaos.

Wolves were tearing at the snake's thick scales in vain and venom sprayed everywhere.

A drop of venom landed on a chocolate brown and a gaping, steaming hole of rotting black flesh opened in between his shoulder blades.

It fell to its knees, writhing in pain as the venom spread.

I gulped.

"That looks nasty, not to mention painful. Do you really want to do this?" a soft and timid female voice said.

"Uh..." my answer was cut off as Charlotte let out another howl.

"Ash! No!" she screamed.

"Her brother," the male voice whispered.

"Question: Before I die, I'd like to know who the hell you are!" I thought.

"Haven't you guessed? We're your instincts!"

"Great. My instincts talk."

"We have names, too!" A new 'instinct' piped in. I rolled my eyes. Lilly froze at the sound of Charlotte's howl and the message it carried. Her pelt bristled and her lips pulled back from dagger-like teeth. You could almost hear the steam whistling out of her ears.

For such a tiny thing she had a lot of power. Her lupine form was as minute in size as her human form, so it was surprising when, as she took in a deep breath, she doubled, then tripled in size. When she took another breath, she tripled in size once again! Lilly was now almost a quarter of the Basak's height and still growing. The Basak didn't notice this at first as it was too busy watching the other wolves slide off it and slink away, smug lupine looks in their faces.

Lilly attacked the Basak, her now long fangs able to tear through the Basak's thick skin. This didn't last long.

She managed to damage its left eye until it was almost blind. That was a mistake.

In its fury and pain the Basak went ballistic. Swinging its head back and forth, its front fang pierced Lilly's shoulder before she could get away. Her form shimmered for a moment before she slid to the ground, human.

There was a shocked silence.

I had started to like Lilly and it angered me to see what this overgrown pathetic excuse for a reptile did to ... my ... kind. Terrified as I was, I launched myself from the tree and onto the Basak's head. Hissing and screaming, it smacked against trees and rolled all over the place trying to get me off.

My stomach began rolling around and trying to push out my insides. I got a brief glimpse of Lilly, her body glistening with sweat, her eyes rolled back so all you could see was the whites. I already had my claws deep in the Basak's red scales - when I saw what this thing's venom could do they were pushed in even deeper.

I looked around and came up with a plan. As the Basak swung past the remaining wolves I gave a small bark, careful not to bite my tongue off. At first they were confused and then they understood. Circling the maddened Basak, they took turns to claw and nip the Basak as it swung by.

The Basak became distracted, trying to get at each wolf as it laid waste to its once protective scales. This gave me the chance to crawl along the Basak's back, exploring for soft patches. Just below the head, facing the sky, was a thinner layer of scales than the others. I pulled all my claws out of the Basak's back and swiped at the vulnerable skin.

Ignoring its agonized screams, I kept digging into the skin. The scales tore away, exposing the soft tissue below.

I didn't stop there.

The tissue ripped easily, but blood kept oozing out and I couldn't find what I was looking for.

"What are you looking for?" an instinct asked.

"Nerves," I replied simply.

"Well, I don't suppose you realized that you are damaging thousands of them or anything?" he asked, politely covering bad sarcasm.

"But not the nerve I'm looking for."

I hit bone at last.

Pushing my paws around the bone, I found a thick white cord with my claws and tugged.

It froze.

Only then did I notice Charlotte gripping onto the Basak's head, her paws covered in blood, the Basak's eyes in ruins. In front of her was a huge lump of flesh, pinkish red in color, throbbing softly. Its heart.

Unfortunately, the heart was still connected to the body, so the Basak wasn't dead. In as much pain as it was, it rolled over, crushing me and Charlotte under its weight. There was a cracking, tearing and popping noise and then, still struggling to breathe, I pulled hard on the cord and there was more tearing, followed by a whooshing noise as air escaped the cord.

I didn't pay attention to these as I was too busy concentrating on the facts that:

A: I couldn't breathe, and

B: I couldn't feel my leg.

I tried moving it and screamed. I felt my flesh tearing where a horn had pierced it. I bit down onto my paw until I tasted blood.

It seemed like forever before I finally managed to lift the Basak's body up enough to squeeze out. I screamed again as the horn tore at my leg. Seven wolves were lifting the Basak off of Charlotte and only when I screamed did they notice that I needed help.

I hadn't noticed until now but a lot of the wolves were either injured or dead. If I had to make a list of top ten worst injuries, Lilly would be eighth next to Ash and some random wolf who was about to die in about five seconds because there just so happened to be spikes pinning him to an aging oak.

Lilly's shoulder wound was festering and green, tinged puss swelled over the sides. Her veins were visible beneath the sweating skin, green with the poison pumping through them. I took in a deep, shaky breath and looked around. I counted 10 injured and five dead.

"I'm sorry, pup. You can go. I forgot that you had a choice whether or not to join us. You would have been a really valuable addition to the pack. You are a very rare breed, even if you are a mutt, or, in more polite terms, mortal born." Charlotte was deeply shaken, that much was obvious.

"I'll sleep on it. For now, you'll need some help getting everybody home," I said, gesturing to those unfit to make it back alone. A look of defeat crashed onto her face, leaving a pang in my chest.

At that moment I felt a prickling sensation on my injured leg, and, looking down, gasped. There was no wound, just a faint and steadily fading pink scar where the wound had been.

"I think I'm going to enjoy this," I muttered, grinning despite the present situation. Another expression flitted across Charlotte's face. Surprise. "Oh, and by the way, my name is Leah." I said, carefully scooping up Lilly.

# JUMBLED

It was too late for Ash. As Charlotte led me through the trees, Ash gave an agonized shriek and she had to put him down. His eyes came into focus on her face and he whimpered.

"Make it stop! Make it stop!" he moaned, his voice cracking as another shriek ripped through his throat. I didn't know why, but these words stirred something in my memories.

"We will, Ash, we will," Charlotte whispered. His back arched, he took one gasping breath and died.

Charlotte let out a howl, her form ripping viscously into wolf. She must have been pretty pissed off or extremely distraught because if you translated her howls you would notice her swearing at Ash and God, both for being morons.

"Um, Charlotte, in case you hadn't noticed, Lilly is dying here, so it might be a good idea if we could, oh, I don't know, get back to camp!" I said, gesturing to Lilly.

Charlotte just growled. I looked at Lilly and jumped. She was staring at me, her eyes bloodshot, lips cracked, mouth slightly open.

"Help me! Please!" she murmured.

This was seriously creepy, seeing as her black and white striped t-shirt was stained with green puss and blood. The wolves fit to walk were behind us, but one of them, a sandy haired guy in his teens, walked up to me and seeing my scared expression KISSED ME!

My first thought: Why is this dick kissing me? My second thought: Kill him. My third thought: Why? My fourth thought: He's kissing you, you nitwit!

Good point. The argument took about two seconds, so he was still kissing me when my fist slipped up and smacked into his lower jaw. There was a crack and he staggered into a tree, his jaw hanging loosely from the only part of the bone that wasn't shattered. He pushed it into place and it immediately healed.

"Well, I guess you've changed a lot more than I thought. I liked you a lot more when you were human," he joked.

"What do you mean? You knew, know me?" I asked, suddenly very interested, my heart's steady hum faltering.

"What? You don't remember... anything?" he asked, his eyebrows knitting together.

"Nope," I said, turning around and reluctantly picking up Lilly. She was really creeping me out.

"Crazy mutt," she whispered, her eyes closing.

"Uh, yeah, I'll take her back to camp. Somebody has to make sure that Charlotte doesn't commit suicide," he tried to joke and failed.

As he turned around and began ushering Charlotte through the trees I noticed a purple, semicircular scar on his left shoulder. The memory of the wolves fighting popped into my head and I frowned.

"Don't push it away! Embrace it!" an instinct shouted.

I latched onto the memory and pulled it to me. That sucking popping noise came back and there I was - standing in the trees but also trapped beneath strong roots at my feet. I watched myself scream and struggle as I saw the wolves fighting.

Confusing isn't it? The brown wolf over took the grey wolf and limped over to me. But the other wolf wasn't going to give up so easily. He growled and an instant translation popped into my head.

"No! You took my sister! You're not taking Leah!" The brown wolf was about to bite into my arm when the grey wolf leapt onto him and started clawing pathetically at the obviously bigger and stronger wolf's pelt. Once again, he was thrown away and as he hit the nearest tree, he morphed.

It was sandy dude.

I felt a faint pang. It was strange. The pang felt distant, like from a memory. Suddenly, I realized something.

In my human life I was in love with him.

"Michael," I whispered. But like my memories, that love had been destroyed by the venom.

The brown wolf nudged my head away from my shoulder and bit down carefully. I started screaming.

"Well, that was pleasant." I thought, once I was out of my memory.

"At least your creation was pleasant," Memory said.

"Wait! Memory? How did I know your name?" I thought.

"It's very easy to put names in your head," Memory said, an image of a young male grinning at me springing into my head.

"Is that so?" I asked, irritated.

"Yup."

"Greeeaat. Just perfect." I felt a warm hand on my shoulder and someone was next to me. He was a guy of around 14, with long brown and bronze streaked hair tied back in a leather band. He was also muscled, but not hectically. His blue and white striped shirt was a little bit big for him and his jeans were faded.

"It's Leah, right?" his voice was smooth, as warm as his touch and husky.

"Uh, yeah." I said. My voice was a little higher than usual and my heart kept fluttering. He raised his eyebrows when he heard its reaction. (His radar ears would obviously pick up the sound.) I swallowed and straightened up.

"What about yours?" I asked.

"Who wants to know?" he grinned, making his whole face light up.

"You're looking at her," I said, my voice betraying me again.

He chuckled.

"Good enough. My name is Kyle Wood," he said, offering his hand to shake.

"Uh, cool," I muttered, starting to walk away.

"Hey, aren't you joining the pack?" Kyle called.

"I said that I'd sleep on it." I said over my shoulder.

" Meaning you're going to sleep at the camp," he said.

I jumped. I hadn't heard his approach. Kyle's warm hand was once again on my shoulder. I was getting irritated.

"No, I'm finding or making a den," I said, reluctantly sliding away from his hand.

"In the camp," he said, taking my arm and steering me in the opposite direction.

"Outside." I growled.

"Outside Lilly's den." Kyle said. He was enjoying this.

"Outside as in the forest." I wormed away and began to jog in the opposite direction.

"Hey, I don't think that is such a good idea," he called after me.

"And why would you care?" I shouted, spinning around.

"Lilly is my... friend. I think I would feel a tiny bit grateful that you saved her fluffy butt," he said.

I jumped again. He had been right behind me the whole time.

"I didn't save her fluffy butt. I was going to kill that thing, get her back to camp and then maybe *your* pack would leave me alone."

Kyle ran in front of me, forcing me to stop.

"Uh, yeah, like that's ever going to happen. Okay, two options: One, you spend the night willingly at camp, or I kick you there." There was a joking threat in his voice.

I glared at him and then sprung to the side, trying to escape under his arm. He stepped to the side, obscuring my escape.

"Well, I guess you're going to have to kick me there," my voice had adopted an icy tone. A breeze whipped up the forest air and my stomach growled.

"You're hungry. You can get a free meal at camp." Kyle said, once again, blocking my second attempt at escaping.

"I hunt for myself." I said as I ducked down and knocked his legs from underneath him, hopping over him and jogging away.

"Why are you so reluctant to accept hospitality?" Kyle panted, tired and exasperated at last.

"I had a rough creation. I don't remember much of my human life. I think I have a right to be suspicious." My voice melted a little bit.

"The world isn't as harsh as you think," he muttered.

"You're wrong. It's harsh and cruel and soulless." My voice went cold again and I stopped so I could shout in his face. The moon shone briefly onto us, highlighting a shoulder wound and fading pink scar on Kyle's leg.

"There's your proof," I pointed at the damage done by the Basak.

"No, that is called a giant snake with s*** attitude," Kyle said, grinning again.

"You wouldn't understand," I grumbled.

"Hey, you're the pup. I was born wolf," he said, his grin stretching across his face, lighting up his face.

I sighed.

They placed me in the 'guest room/den'. The guest room was a big underground room with smooth sandstone walls and a soft fur bed.

It was torture. It took me about two minutes when inside to realize that my worst fear was being trapped. I kept wondering what would happen if I was attacked.

"Don't worry! We won't be attacked. These are nice wolves," Trust, my newest instinct said.

"Shut up!" I thought.

"Now, now Leah, is that any way to speak to Trust?" Manners reprimanded me.

"If you had a mouth I would recommend you shut it," I thought back viciously.

"Now, now Leah..." she was cut off as I pushed her to the back of my head. I had been here for who knows how long and had been too occupied with being trapped, or too tired to sleep. I sat down and instantly leapt up again. What I had sat on had moved. I turned in time to see what I had thought was a pillow, get up. I raised my eyebrows as I saw what I had sat on.

"I know some pretty desperate gals, but boy you are bad at this," the man said, his fur coat ruffled and words slurred under the influence of drink. "What are you doing 'ere?" he asked once he had smoothed out his coat.

"I was just about to ask the same thing, sir," I said, the last word in sarcasm.

He growled at me. "I just so happen to live here," he shouted.

"Well that's a shocker because I'm a prisoner here," I replied.

"Ha! Newbie, 'ey?" he spat on the floor at my feet and wiped his mouth on his hand. I looked down at the white glob at my feet and frowned.

"Don't do that please." My voice was calm, but I knew what was coming.

He repeated the act of spitting at my feet and rubbing it into the ground. His breath stank as he pushed his face closer to mine.

"What you gonna do about it, chicky?" he whispered, placing his hands on my hips.

"Get your hands off me," I whispered, clenching my fists.

"Why? Scared of lil old Ricky?" he said, leaning up and trying to kiss me. An instinct completely new to me gripped my control and one moment I was trapped, the next I was behind him and my fist collided with his ear. With a grunt, "Ricky" hit the wall.

His thin ginger hair seemed brighter as the blood drained from his face and sweat beaded his brow. Scraping his heels against the floor, "Ricky" pushed himself against the wall.

I walked up to him, took a fistful of his shirt and lifted him off the ground. He yelped and kicked, trying to struggle free.

"You're a female! You can't do this!" he screamed.

"Is that so? Watch me, darling." I said, a vicious smile spreading across my face.

It gave me a strange sense of satisfaction to watch him flying airborne across the corridor and smacking against the opposite side. Whimpering, Ricky curled up in a fetal position and moaned, "Bitch."

"A Bitch and proud of it too," I said, kicking him in the crotch and then walking back inside the guest room, the door banging loudly behind me.

Heads popped out of their rooms to see what was going on and a female called out: "Woo! You go, girl!" after me. My decision was final.

The way things worked in the camp was quite satisfactory. Mated wolves lived in pairs in the underground tunnels and unmated wolves lived in dens above ground, females in the trees and males on the ground. This was so if there was a battle the females or VIPP's (Very Important Pup Producers) wouldn't get hurt at first. Living in the trees as a pack member, separated from the males and free, life was rather uneventful.

Even though I was a part of the pack I didn't depend on it. I built my den by myself, hunted for myself, took care of myself.

So it was a real surprise when I heard a knock on the branch outside my den. I lived in a large pine tree, just outside the mated tunnels.

I had been in the middle of finishing off my roof, (I had only been in the pack for two days), when I heard the knock.

I walked across the woven floor and to the opening of my den. Kyle was hanging from a branch, his arms wrapped over it and his feet dangling below so as not to fall, his tanned face bright red from the effort of trying to get up.

I laughed for the first time since my creation and said, "I may be a pup, but at least I can climb a tree."

"Ha, ha, ha, very funny, now can you please help me up?" His voice was choked with strain.

I laughed again and, taking his hand, began pulling him inside my den. We sat there puffing for a moment, Kyle from the climb, me from laughing.

It took me a moment to realize that I was leaning against him and quickly got up.

"So what's big bad older wolf doing in the pack pup's den?" I asked, forcing a smile.

He hesitated.

The moonlight swept through the clearing and glinted off Kyle's long hair.

I lost myself for a moment and suddenly realized that I was taking in the details of his broad, tanned shoulders and almost adult-like face.

"I guess I wanted to see you," he finally said.

"Uh, why?" I asked, turning around and walking across the den. My cheeks had kidnapped all my blood and were red and hot. I was blushing!

I walked to the centre of the room and waited.

No need. Kyle was right behind me.

"Lilly is healing well, thanks to Healer Neleh. Ash was buried yesterday and..." his voice trailed off.

"Is that all?" I asked.

"Uh, I was wondering when you were going to find a ma... I mean a mentor," he quickly changed the direction of his question when he saw my expression.

I was glaring at him.

"What were you going to say?" I asked, teeth clenched.

"Mentor. I was going to say mentor," he said, looking me straight in the eye.

"Really?" I injected tons of ice into my glare, pushing it to him. He stood his ground.

"What do I need a mentor for?" It was a casual question but none of the ice had left.

"To train you. What else?" Kyle shrugged. He had obviously learnt to stay warm and guilt free.

Clever Bastard.

"What would he or she train me in?" I asked. I had given up my hostile stand and gone back to having a conversation.

"Fighting and hunting," he smiled.

"I bet I could beat you any day." It was a joke but he seemed to take me seriously.

"You're on," he said, looking me in the eye.

"Just for the record before, kicking your sorry butt, why would I need training to defend myself?" I had pushed my face right up close to him.

He seemed almost panicked to have me so close to him. Kyle took a step back and began to walk away.

"Bitches in packs don't get respect easily. They have to work twice as hard and earn it," he said over his shoulder and dived out the door.

I walked across the den and looked out onto the night:

Clear, though my emotions were not.

# BATTLE

Emotions are so strange. They fight for control over you and when they get control, mess up your life.

Metaphorically speaking, lemons were turned onto my cuts and made my life a nightmare. Whenever I saw Kyle I would blush and go quiet. It was kind of annoying and I tried to keep myself busy to avoid free minutes.

Two emotions were battling each other, Regret and Love. I was on Regret's side, but Love was stubborn and wouldn't give up. The dream I was having every night was killing my nine precious hours of sleep. They all started the same.

I was in a clearing rimmed by boulders and high slopes. Dead and dry grass covered the ground and small thorn trees dotted the field, their branches bare and reaching for the sky. Kyle would be running towards me, calling to me. All of a sudden Ash would appear next to me and watch as Kyle suddenly fell to the ground.

Arrows stuck out of his back and he would lie there, writhing in pain and calling to me. Time would be harsh as I struggled to get to him. My legs were too heavy and I couldn't get there in time. A huge black wolf leapt from the top of one of the slopes and start tearing at Kyle, ignoring his screams of agony.

Ash took my arm and looked me in the eye.

His voice went raspy and he started looking like he did when he died. Ash grabbed me by my shoulders and held me in a grip of steel, repeating these words.

"On the eve of Cactay,
a dear price you will pay.
Soon death will be what you seek,
all within a week.
As the sun sets on the seventh day
you will know that you've been betrayed
by one who calls friend.
All ends will be frayed
and only then,
will death be paid."

Then he withered up and I'd wake up screaming.

Though I knew it was only a dream, I would creep into Kyle's den and check that he was okay.

He would always be asleep, unharmed. Tonight was especially bad. I tip-toed into his den and nearly freaked. He wasn't there. Trying to be rational, I tried to come up with an explanation. That didn't help. I walked into his den and began to wonder. I had never known this feeling. Walking to the back of the room I saw a small wooden picture frame. Inside it was a picture of Lilly and Kyle, smiling, his hands around her waist. I felt a flash of jealousy that took me by surprise.

"What are you doing here?"

I nearly jumped out of my skin when I heard Kyle's husky voice in my ear. I turned around, trying to see where he was and nearly ran right into him. I tried to wriggle away, but his strong hands grabbed my arms so I couldn't get away.

"How can I get out of here with you holding onto me?" I spat.

"Jeez, hold onto your hair! I think I have a right to know what you are doing in my room?" Kyle said, smiling.

I scowled. "Water. I was thirsty and wondered straight in here by accident because the stupid moon wouldn't show its face." I wriggled free and walked to the den entrance.

There was a gentle breeze and he leaned casually against the entrance frame, his legs crossing over the other side, blocking my escape.

"Don't lie, Leah! Every night you are in here, checking on me when I'm supposedly asleep." Kyle's gaze felt questioning.

Silence.

He gently took my arm and towed me out the door. I followed reluctantly, biding my time.

"Villain," Trust grumbled sleepily. I smiled.

Kyle was confused as my expression changed from a smile to concentration and back again. I was wrestling with Trust as she fought to take over.

"Why do you do that?" he asked, his steady jog never slowing.

"Vivid instincts. Don't have 'em?" I asked, smiling as Trust gave up and slunk to the back of my head to sulk.

"Not in plural," Kyle said, a frown scaring his beautiful, detailed, young, handsome face. As we jogged he always kept one eye peeking at me from the corner. This made me blush crimson and I thanked the lord that it was too dark for him to see my face.

"So, where are we going?" I asked.

"Don't change the subject."

"What subject?"

"Why do you check on me every night?" He had stopped.

"Nightmares."

"So you admit it!"

"Mmmm."

"And the nightmares are about me?"

"Mmmm hmm."

"What happens?" he asked, a strong sense of curiosity clear in his voice.

"You die, I get a prophecy and wake up screaming." My smile was full of dark humor.

"Uh huh, and you would care about me - why?" He was cautious, almost gleeful.

I sprang to the side, nailing Kyle beneath me and kept my hands on his arms so he couldn't get away.

"If a bitch can catch you off guard, then I should be worried," I whispered in his ear.

Kyle reached for my face, but I was gone. The wind in my face, the smell of the forest, hair flying behind my shoulders and the thrill of the chase was on. He was always right behind me, on my heels, laughing as I managed to keep out of his grasp.

A cliff came into view, strong and black, looming over the fast moving waters below. It was like flying as I fell through the air, Kyle hesitating on the cliff above.

The landing was like a bullet slicing through water, a cloud of bubbles streaming behind. Water filled my mouth and nose and soon my lungs were screaming for air. My head broke the surface just as Kyle let out a WHOOP! and hit the water, making a wave wash over my head.

It was hard for him, but Kyle finally caught me. I had taken a rough turn and he had grabbed my arm before I could fall and get away from him again. We lay next to each other, panting and laughing. He sat up and looked at me.

"Why would you care if I died?" Kyle asked, his eyes light and questioning, concealing an eager sparkle.

"I don't know," I shrugged.

It was a completely honest answer. The blushing, the nightmares, none of it made any sense to me at the time and they still didn't as I said those words.

"Try," he said, taking my hand.

"I... why would you care?" I was suddenly angry at myself and him for making me feel this way and I ripped my hand from his.

"I can't tell," he said slyly.

"Show me then!" I said stubbornly sitting up and folding my arms tightly across my chest. Most of that had been Love and I silently cursed her.

Kyle's hands grasped my face gently and pulled me close to him. He leant forward and whispered, "With your permission," in my ear. He took my silence as a yes and leant down, pressing his soft lips onto mine. A fire burst between us and I lost control, throwing my hands around his neck, pulling him closer. He didn't object and twined his hands into my hair. Emotions went wild, not allowing each other to overthrow the vicious love that I now felt beating in every single vein in my body.

Kyle seemed to be having the same war and pulled me onto his lap, holding me as close to him as possible. The kiss molded us together and we became one. His arms wrapped around my waist and held me tightly to him. I gasped for air and his lips brushed along my jaw, painting them with fire. I knew what was happening, but I didn't care. I pushed against his chest and kissed him long and fast. He gripped my face and soon was on his back. I didn't want the night to end.

I woke up the next morning, warm and feeling strangely satisfied. The whole night flashed in slides before me and I sighed as the familiar fire crawled back into my skin.

I heard a soft chuckle.

"You look very proud of yourself," Kyle said, turning his head to look at me.

"Proud?" I asked rolling over to look at him.

"Wrong word?" he asked, his voice thick with sarcasm.

"Humph. There goes my virginity," I muttered, the frost below me crunching as I rolled over again, turning my back to Kyle.

A tingle rushed up my spine and into my cheeks as he started tracing zig-zag patterns on my shoulder. Feeling a little too comfortable I sat up and began studying his face - how his dark brown hair caught the light and glinted bronze. I stared at my olive toned hands and started thinking about my age when a thought struck me.

My eyes traveled along my side, tracing the hip bone and came to rest on my navel. An image of a half-formed human foetus popped into my head and I suppressed a shudder. Kyle seemed to have had the same thought because he suddenly sat up and began listening hard. I glanced at him before flipping the imaginary switch between human and wolf hearing. The booming thud of our hearts and the deafening roar of the blood rushing through our veins rang in my ears, but there was no sign of a third heart. Breathing a sigh of relief, Kyle stood up and brushed the dirt off of his pants and shirt before reaching out to me. I took his hand but pulled him down instead of him pulling me up. Laughing, I jumped up and ran away, calling, "Catch me if you can!" over my shoulder.

The sky was lightening as we made our way back to camp. I stopped and trailed my hand away from Kyle's, walking to the top of a small hill. It felt a little bit melodramatic but I sank to my knees and sat there, watching the sunrise.

"It's the only thing that stays the same in my life," I said as Kyle joined me.

"You don't remember being human?" he asked, his voice brimming with curiosity.

"No," I replied.

"Your parents, your house, nothing?" Kyle asked, his surprise mingled with pity.

"Why would you care?" I asked jokingly.

"I need to know my enemy from the inside out for when I battle them," he said, the grin I loved so much spreading over his face.

I was silent.

Then suddenly I leapt onto Kyle, turning into a gleaming, white wolf at the last minute, knocking him to the ground.

His surprise didn't last long and he shifted into a beautiful brown wolf, his pelt gleaming. This distracted me and he flipped me over so that I was beneath him. Kyle's stomach was white and exposed. Using my back legs, claws sheathed, I kicked up, sending him flying.

The strangest feeling washed over me and I slid to the ground, watching as his muscles glided smoothly into place, his legs rebounding off a tree. He did a graceful spin in midair and came flying in my direction. I leapt into the air and spun, copying his movements. I twisted over him, grazing my paws along his back. Just before I passed over him completely, I gripped onto Kyle's shoulders.

With both of us spinning, we collided together and tumbled to the floor. He was beneath me and I put my hand over his heart and whispered "Dead" in his ear, before getting up and walking away.

"I think I just got pulverized by a bitch," I heard him say, followed closely by a laugh.

# WAR

It was cold and grey, dew barely visible on the blades of grass and leaves on the trees. Frost melted below foot as the heat of the soldiers walked over it. No weapons were visible. (There was no need of them.) On the other side of the field, soldiers, all with their hair long and red streaks painted on their bare arms and chests like scratches, emerged from the trees. Peter stood and watched as they moved out onto the field, ready for a battle to the death. Muscles tensed, eyes closed, he started thinking of his baby girl, Angelica and his fiance, Miyandrea. If he died in this battle, he would never get to look into those beautiful tiger stone eyes again and Angelica would never know her father.

"Attack!" Gabrielle, the pack leader, shouted, his booming voice drowned out by the cries of wolves as every man shed his human appearance and took the form of their brothers and sisters, the wolves.

Fur went flying as wolves swarmed over each other, biting and scratching. Peter was instantly attacked by three wolves and was outmatched. He killed them, but his chest and underbelly were bleeding profusely and his lower back had snapped. Now he had no use of his back legs. A picture of Angelica, her beautiful brown eyes gleaming with intelligence, her cocoa brown hair long and shining, popped into his head and he found strength flowing into his every limb.

He began fighting more and more viciously, killing as many wolves as he could get his paws on. As he dragged a white wolf off of his brother, a shadow fell over him. Orlando struck and Peter fell to the floor.

As he died, a howl ripped through the air and Miyandrea picked up a knife, ready to slit her throat.

# LOVE

I woke up screaming and instantly Kyle pulled me close to him and started whispering reassurance into my ear. He was there; it was just a nightmare; it was okay. We heard a shriek. I sat up and looked through the den entrance.

Lilly stood in the doorway, her large eyes filled with betrayal, wild, her hair no longer bouncing with the rest of her body. She opened her mouth to scream again, but Kyle had his hand clamped tightly over her mouth.

"Is the idea of me and Lee that terrifying?" he grumbled as Lilly started to collapse, her eyes never leaving Kyle's face. He slowly let go of her and she lunged at him, pinning him to the wall. Tears welled up in her eyes and spilled over as she started to strangle him.

"You f***** bastard! You filthy piece of s***!" she screamed, banging his head against the wall. He started to go blue by the time I managed to get her attention by nailing her in the eye with my takkie. She threw Kyle against the opposite wall, placing both hands around his neck and squeezing. I picked up my shoe and nailed her temple in an attempt to break her hold. Lilly screamed and threw him across the room, diving at me and pinning me to the ground.

I punched her jaw as she started to block off my air ways. Stars started popped in my eyes as I struggled to loosen her hold, at the same time trying to keep my fingers pressed into her morphasion nerve.

Suddenly, Lilly's hands where gone and I managed to take a deep breath.

"Chill it, Tiny!" A high voice commanded.

I propped myself up on my elbows to take a look at the new arrival.

She was a tall, slender, fragile teenager. In the dim light, I could barely see her but I managed to make out bronze hair and tiger stone eyes that changed color.

"Angelica! What the hell?" Kyle moaned.

"What? I don't get a thank you?" Angelica said, cracking Lilly's head on the night stand to knock her out.

Kyle chuckled, breathed a sigh of relief, and relaxed. I didn't trust her, but relaxed anyway.

Trust wanted to know how long she had known about me and Kyle, but she was pushed away. My dream about Miyandrea and Peter in the clearing, naming their unborn (now born) daughter popped into my head.

"Her name will be Angelica, Dew that Glistens in the Morning Sun."

"Uh, Angelica, what is your wolf name?" I asked.

"Dew that Glistens in the Morning Sun, or Dew for short. Why?" she asked, confused.

I gulped, my mouth dry. "Who's... your mom?" I asked, my voice cooler than I could possibly imagine. Hopes were building in my chest. She may be my link to my human life! And then she burst my bubble.

"No idea. My mom dropped me off outside Healer Neleh's den and left a note saying that my dad had died in a war and it pained her that I looked so much like him. She told Neleh my name and that's it."

The hopes exploded in my chest and my expression dropped.

"Wow. I'm sorry. I don't remember my parents." I said.

"Ditto." Kyle replied.


It was a cold night, perfect for snooping. Nobody guarded the camp entrance so it was easy to get out. There were no pine needles to make noise and traveling through the trees was much more fun. A wolf's nose can detect pretty much anything so it was easy to find the nearest human settlement. A man, around about 42 or younger, was gardening by moonlight. His hands moved shakily over the ground as he pulled out weeds and pried vegetables out of the ground.

"Dad!" A voice whimpered. There was no pause in the movement from blue-eyed, white-furred wolf to Indian girl. Sliding to the ground was easy, it was the approach that was the hard part.

He, no doubt about it, would freak out when he saw his supposedly dead daughter. There was no need to approach. James saw the girl in the shadows and ran forward. He tripped over the fence and turned, running back into his house. Like I had predicted, he had obviously thought that I was a ghost and freaked out.

The fence was no obstacle, but it was a matter of desperation that made it difficult to see the small tombstone in front of the begonias. Tripping and getting a mouth full of dirt won't put you in a good mood! Before a blow could shatter the square of granite, words caught my eye.

*Leah Surely*
*March 21st, 1997 - March 22nd, 1997*

I raised my eyebrows in shock. Written below it was a surprising message.

"God bless our first attempt at a child," I read aloud.

"She died a day after birth. We should have told you sooner." James said.

I turned around and came face to face with him.

"No! I am your daughter. I have to be!" I said, panicked.

"No, Leah, I'm so sorry. We adopted you. Arian was so desperate to have a child!" he tried to reach for me, but I stepped away.

"Who am I, James?" I whispered.

"Leah," he choked.

"Who am I?" I repeated.

"Leah!" he screamed.

"Who are my parents?" my voice was dangerously calm. Anger and shock had taken control and I began to shake.

"I am! I raised you!" James whimpered.

"Tell me!" I shrieked, grabbing his collar and lifting him off the ground.

"Please!" he moaned.

"Tell me!" I screamed again.

"Okay, okay! Your name was Robin. Your parents died in an animal attack! Please, don't kill me!" he was almost hysterical.

I flung him to the ground and let out an inhuman shriek. Taking deep breaths, I shakily morphed and slammed through the fence and into the forest. Running was always calming: The steady thud of my feet and the only responsibility was to make sure you didn't hit a tree. In this case, I just ran.

"It's too late to apologize!" I wanted to scream.

"Turn back!" Trust and Courtesy were literally shrieking at me.

"Shut up! Leave me alone!" I waited as they went silent. I didn't notice Kyle until I smashed right into him. The impact made me gasp and I was forced to morph.

"Leah! Are you okay?" he asked, panicked.

"Don't call me that! It's not my name!" I shouted, running away.

"Leah!" Kyle called.

"Robin!" James shouted.

"Come back, please!" they both shouted.

Wind, leaves and branches whipped along the way, but finally the cliff came into view. Morphasion was smooth and a howl arose. Being on the edge of the cliff, a thrill raced the anger. It was the new moon and the howl escaped. It was a jagged noise that tore at your heart and chilled the bone. It was the sound of sorrow, success, loneliness and even victory. It expressed the anger and hurt that builds up inside you. The wildest feeling fills the holes in you and makes you want to run.

Wind whipped fur and howls constantly escaped as the forest opened up to this enraged beast. Blood gushed and several forest deer and rabbits fell victim to an empty stomach. One antelope fought too hard to live and was shredded under inch long claws. Running faster and further, there was plenty of time to think. Days flew by and soon I couldn't even remember ever being in human form. Humans had too vivid emotions, uncontrollable desires and wishes. Kyle was the only thing that stuck. His lips on mine was unforgettable and I finally flopped to the ground, too tired to sleep, too confused to think. His soft skin, his warm, husky voice, his hands that painted fire on my skin and made tingles rush up and down my spine. The camp. Food. Love. Grief. Anger. Mine. All mine.

My scent was not hard to track and camp was soon in sight. Nobody was around and the scent was stale. Kyle's den was empty, as was mine. Angelica's, Lilly's (not that I would care!) everybody's. Gone. I morphed slowly and sank to the floor. The sun slowly began to set, turning the sky violet.

The only thing that was reliable. Voices, panicked and reassuring came within earshot. I didn't hear them. Not in a literal way anyway. My head was spinning and my mind shut off. I just sat there, my knees hugged up to my breast, my head in my hands.

"Leah? Leah!" Kyle shouted, using that foul name I had thought was my own.

"Leah, you're okay! Where were?" he didn't finish.

"Don't call me that! It is not my name!" I snapped, not lifting my head.

"What? Leah, what are you talking about?" he asked again.

"That is not my name!" I said, looking up.

"My *parents* lied to me! My name is Robin. They adopted me," my voice sounded choked and I suddenly realized that I was fighting back tears.

I curled back up into my ball and started suppressing sobs. Lilly walked up to me and kicked me.

"You f****** bitch! Look what you've done now!" she hissed.

"I've done nothing!" I shrieked, flinging myself onto her.

" F*****!" she screamed. I pinned her to the ground and wrapped my long fingers around her throat.

It took half an hour, four males and a heck of a lot of rope to get me off of her. My lip was bleeding, but Lilly had a scratched shoulder, 3 or 4 bruises and a bleeding nose. I had ropes around my wrists and legs, holding me back as I struggled to put my hands back in their rightful place. Around her neck.

"Robin! Chill pill!" Angelica said, making a time out sign with her hands.

I stuck my middle finger at Lilly but calmed down anyway.

They took the ropes away, never taking their eyes off me. Kyle scooped me up and walked away. His normal grin was gone and had been replaced by hard anger. I tried to stay in stubborn anger but I just couldn't. He climbed up the hill and laid me down. Just as quickly, he sat me up and taking my jaw, turned my head towards the setting sun.

"The sun doesn't stay with you. It abandons you," he whispered, anger still carved into his face.

"At least I know that it will come back," I said, squirming away from the temptation to kiss him. I was leaving again. I had already hurt him once. I wasn't going to do it again. Never.

"So you're in love with something that ditches you and then comes back?" he asked, a growl in the back of his throat.

"I am *not* in love with a ball of fire. I just ... rely on it."

"If you love me, I'll never, ever, leave you." Kyle wrapped his arms around and I had to build a wall of ice in front of the fire. It didn't work.

"Promise?" I whispered.

"Cross my lupine heart," he replied, taking my face in his hands and kissing me gently. It turned from gentle to vicious and once again we were molded together. Nothing could *ever* pull us apart. As we pulled apart to breath I gasped, "I'm sorry! I will never hurt you again."

"You know you'll have to own up?" he said, still breathless.

"Is this enough?" I whispered, kissing him again, my hands around his neck.

"Mmm, no, but it's a start." Kyle said, cheekily.

"Fine by me." I mumbled, as his lips pressed onto mine.

"This was exactly what we didn't want to happen!" Seek screamed.

"I don't care! Fate's never on my side anyway."

I couldn't leave. Not now. Fortunately, our 'secret' love screwed up my plans to find my parents. Or maybe not so fortunately.

I didn't understand how, but as much as I wanted to find my parents and question them, I couldn't do it without Kyle. The choice was so hard that I couldn't sleep.

I guess that was a good thing.

It was a warm night, but mist still clutched at the ground. The steady thud of large paws hitting the ground and the breath that misted the air was a comfortable rhythm as I paced the camp entrance. War, Comfort and Seek were all on my parent's side of the choice but everyone else wanted to stay.

An all out battle was raging in my head. Everybody was arguing. It was so loud that I didn't hear an approach until Michael gently touched my shoulder. All of my instincts shut up as my head whipped up.

"Robin?" he whispered. I nodded.

"Can we talk?" his voice was shaking.

"Uh, oh." I thought.

"Why did you choose Wood?" Michael asked.

Slipping into human, I turned around and snapped, "That's none of your business!" before turning around and walking away. He zoomed in front of me.

"Tell me, and I'll tell you about the necklace that you are wearing," he said, pointing to the silver wolf hanging around my neck.

"Tempting," I said, and walked away.

"Robin, please... I'm begging you ... plea..." his pleading was abruptly cut off.

There was a crack, rip and a bloodcurdling scream. Whipping around, my stomach began to churn at the grizzly scene meeting my eyes.

"Orlando," I whispered.

Michael was lying on the ground, the left side of his throat ripped out. Blood splattered and pooled on and around his face and head, thick and scarlet. I don't know where the name came from, but all I had to know was Creator + killer = Hate/Orlando. Do the math.

He grinned and then shot into camp, followed by an entire pack of wolves. As I raced to Michael's side, screams and howls began to fill the air.

"Michael, stay alive, please?" I whispered helplessly.

His eyes began to glaze and his dying words were:

"Necklace, answer, love you." His head lolled to the side. A roaring filled my ears and before I knew what was going on, I was inside the camp, sinking my claws into every wolf I could put my paws on.

My eyes were constantly scanning the battle raging around me for my creator. He appeared like lightning, landing on me, claws ripping at fur. I howled in pain and rage, rolling over and over, trying to get rid of him, but he just leapt on me again. An enraged howl and Kyle smashed into Orlando. Bad mistake.

Pinning him down, Orlando began to tear at Kyle's underbelly, dodging his frantic blows.

"Kyle, nooooo!" I howled and lunged at Orlando, bowling him over. My fangs sank into warm flesh and Orlando lay limp below me, dead. Horror clouded my thoughts as I stared at his body, the heat slowly fading from it.

"I killed him." The thought reeled inside my head but no joy followed it. I morphed, staring at my hands, covered in my creator's blood.

For a reason I can't explain, tears rolled down my cheeks.

"Robin, it's over," Kyle choked, his hand pressed down on his wounds. I turned to look at him and smiled weakly as he brushed the tears off of my face.

"No, Robin. Remember the prophecy." Ash and Michael's words chorused in my ears.

My smile faded.

"No," I whispered, looking into Kyle's eyes.

"This is just the beginning."

# About the Author

Jordan van Steenderen was born in June 2000 in Cape Town, South Africa.

Jordan is a free spirited, creative person, with an excellent sense of humor, and is a voracious reader. She started writing her first book in 2009, that she completed in 2011 as *Red Moon* at the age of 11. She has already written the sequel, *Moonlight*, and is currently writing the third book in the series.

Jordan wrote Red Moon, entirely on her own After she finished writing it by hand Jordan typed it up and gave it to her father for publishing. The story was lightly edited for grammar, spelling and punctuation. The story is as she wrote it and the writing style her own.